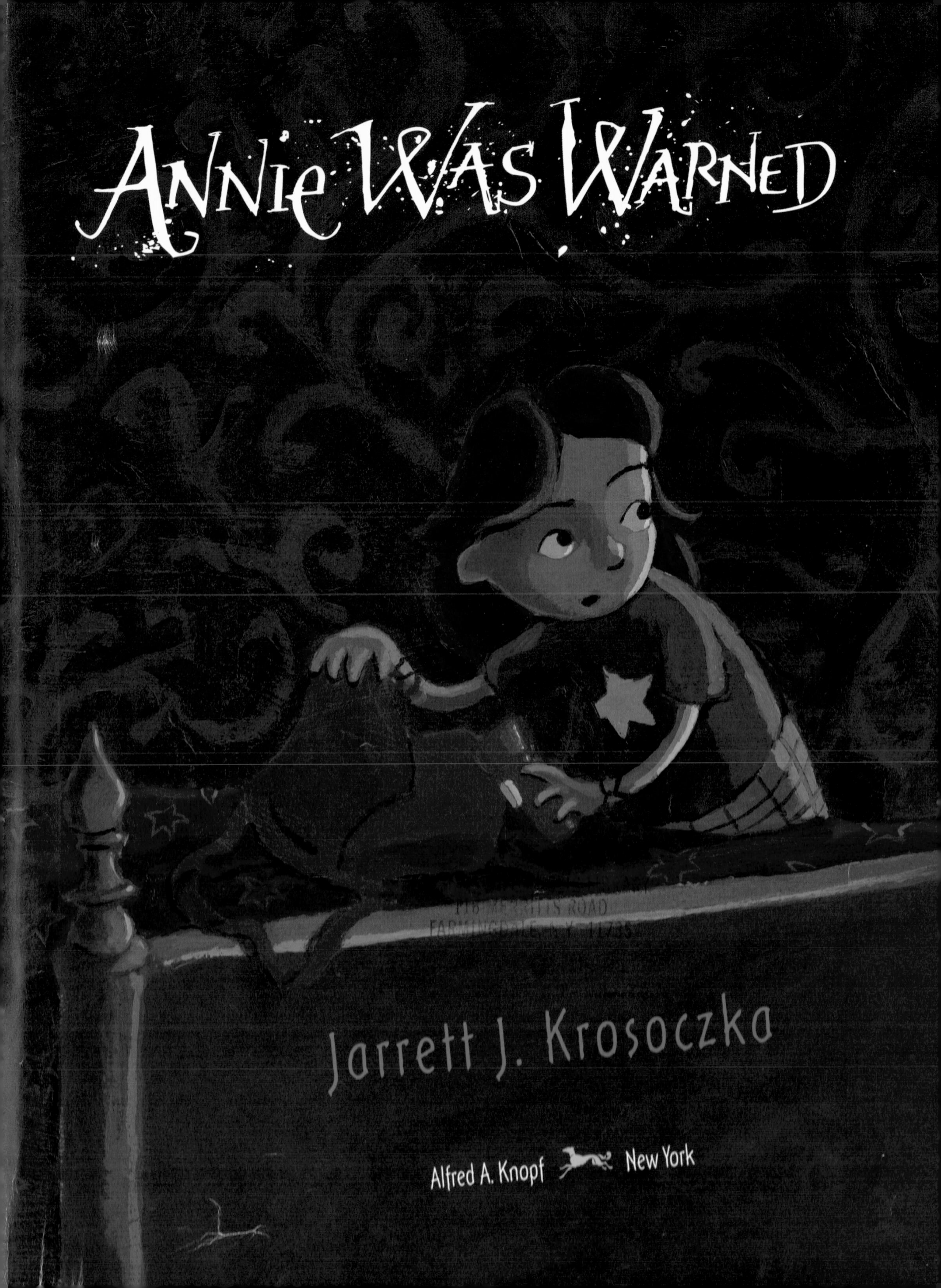

Annie Was Warned

Jarrett J. Krosoczka

Alfred A. Knopf New York

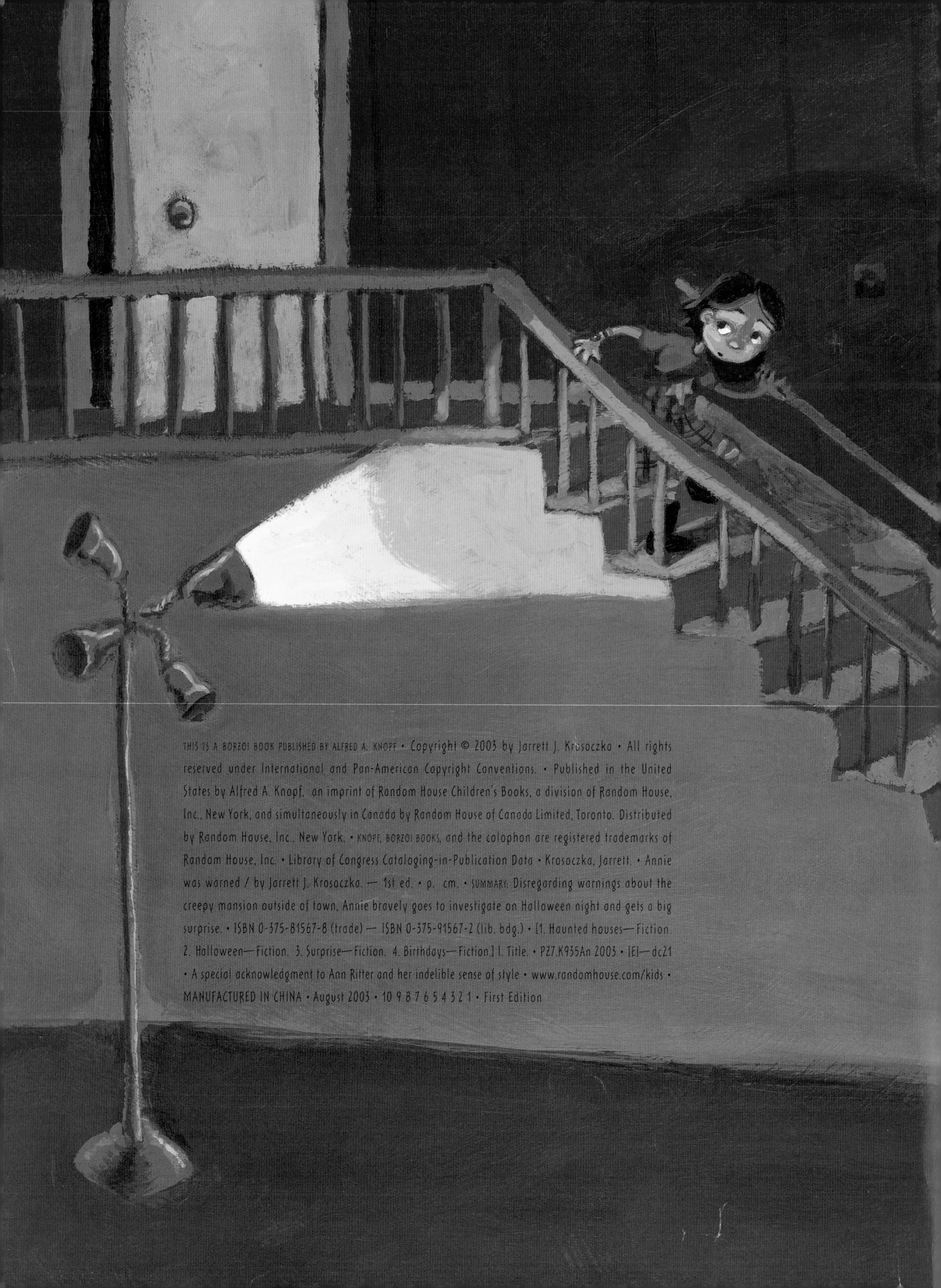

THIS IS A BORZOI BOOK PUBLISHED BY ALFRED A. KNOPF • Published in the United States by Alfred A. Knopf, an imprint of Random House Children's Books, a division of Random House, Inc., New York, and simultaneously in Canada by Random House of Canada Limited, Toronto. Distributed by Random House, Inc., New York. • KNOPF, BORZOI BOOKS, and the colophon are registered trademarks of Random House, Inc. • Library of Congress Cataloging-in-Publication Data • Krosoczka, Jarrett. • Annie was warned / by Jarrett J. Krosoczka. — 1st ed. • p. cm. • SUMMARY: Disregarding warnings about the creepy mansion outside of town, Annie bravely goes to investigate on Halloween night and gets a big surprise. • ISBN 0-375-81567-8 (trade) — ISBN 0-375-91567-2 (lib. bdg.) • [1. Haunted houses—Fiction. 2. Halloween—Fiction. 3. Surprise—Fiction. 4. Birthdays—Fiction.] I. Title. • PZ7.K935An 2003 • [E]—dc21 • A special acknowledgment to Ann Ritter and her indelible sense of style • www.randomhouse.com/kids • MANUFACTURED IN CHINA • August 2003 • 10 9 8 7 6 5 4 3 2 1 • First Edition

For my sister,
Maura

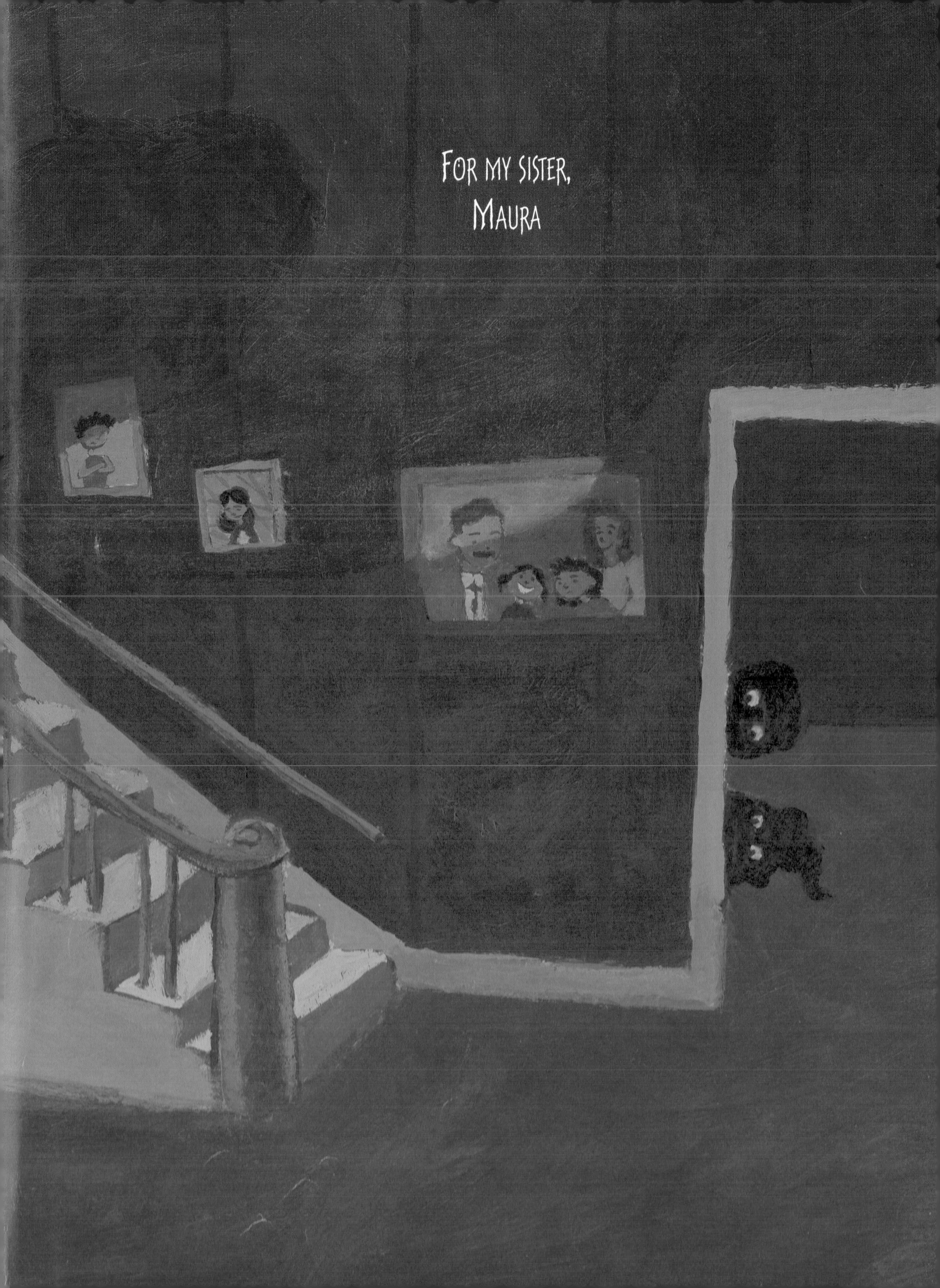

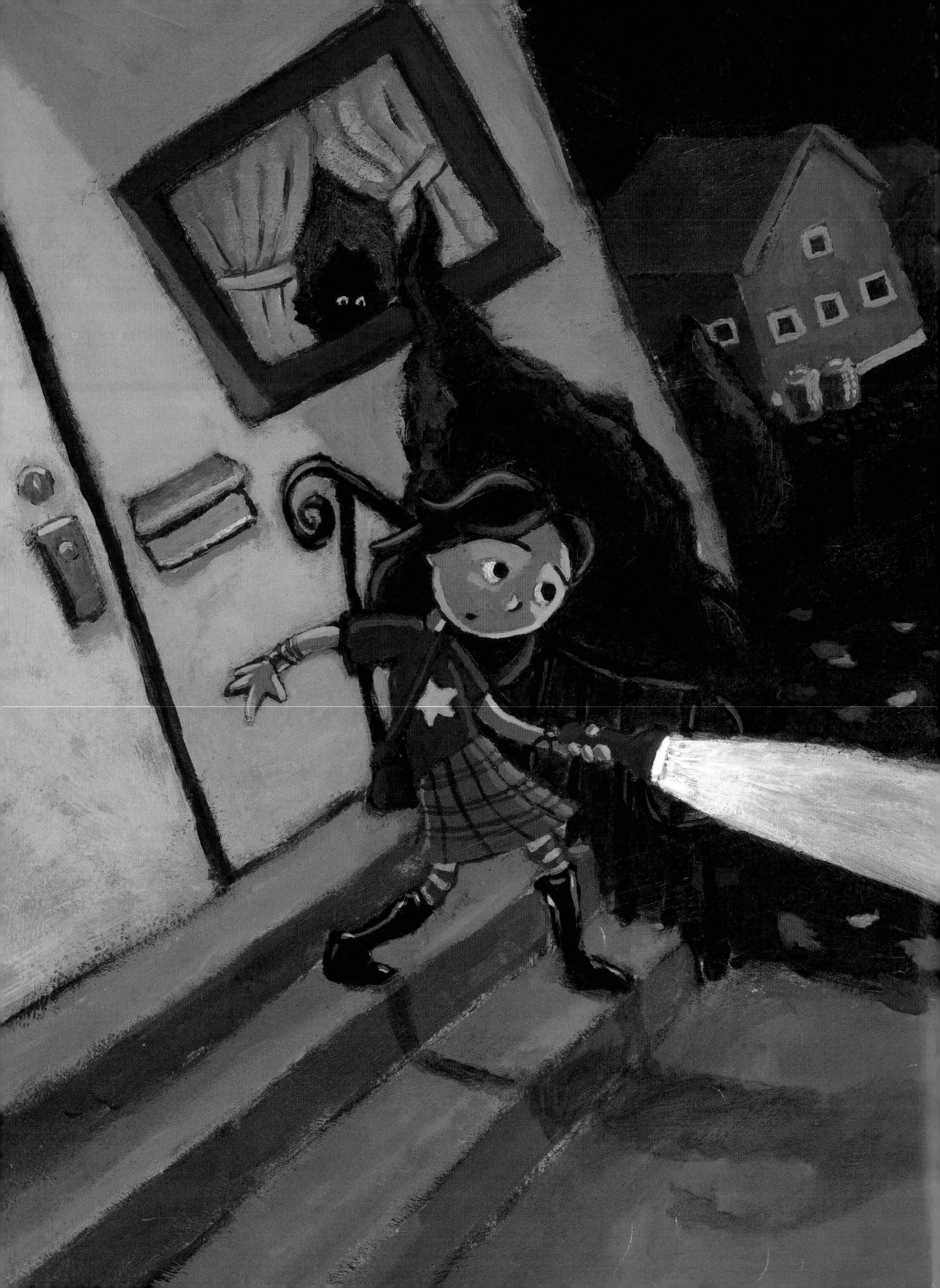

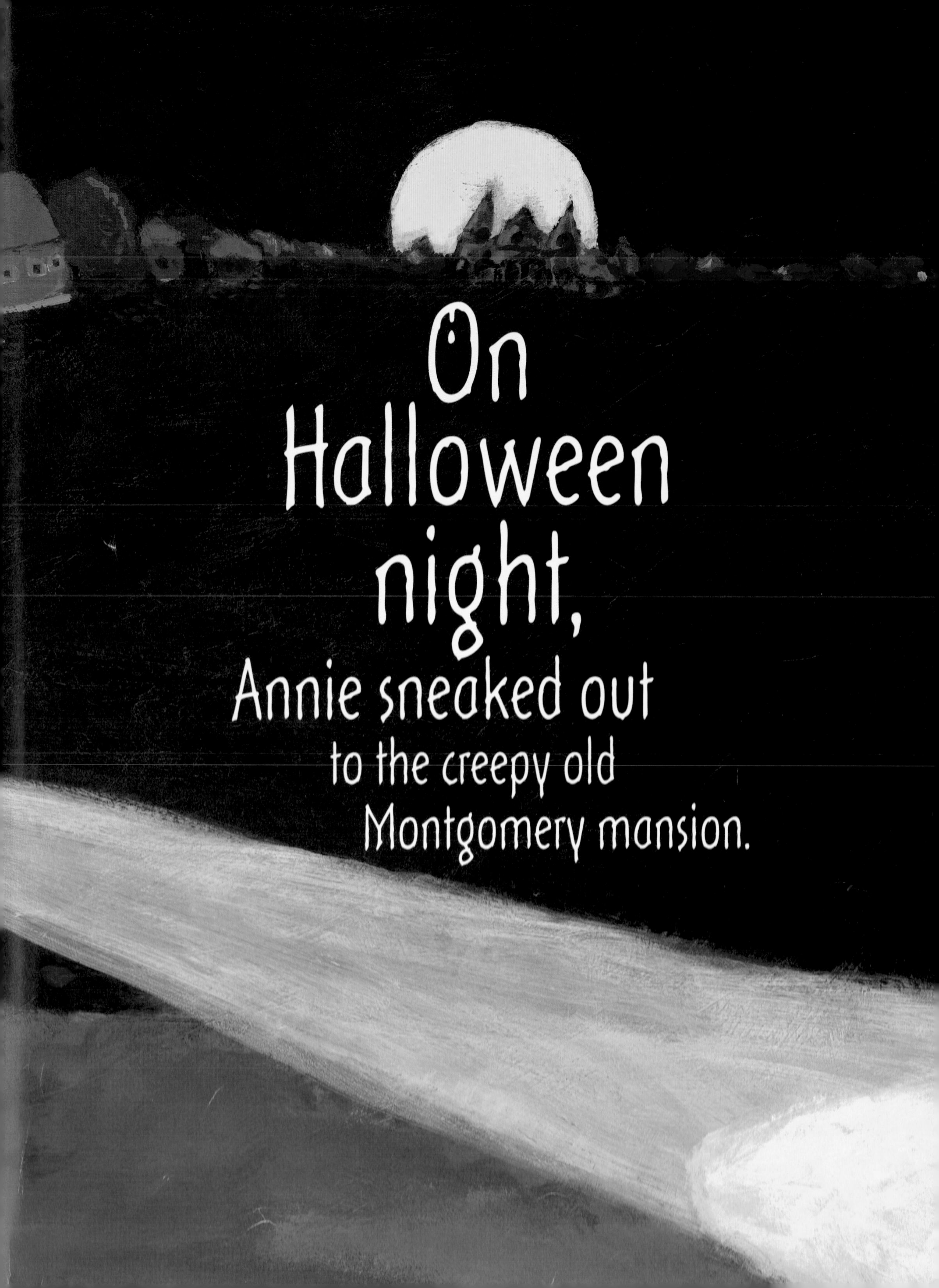

On Halloween night,
Annie sneaked out
to the creepy old
Montgomery mansion.

Annie's parents told her not to go.
"It's got bats," they warned.
     "Bats don't scare me!" Annie said.

Annie's big sister said she
should stay away.
"It's full of creepy spiders,"
she cautioned.
     "I like spiders." Annie smiled.

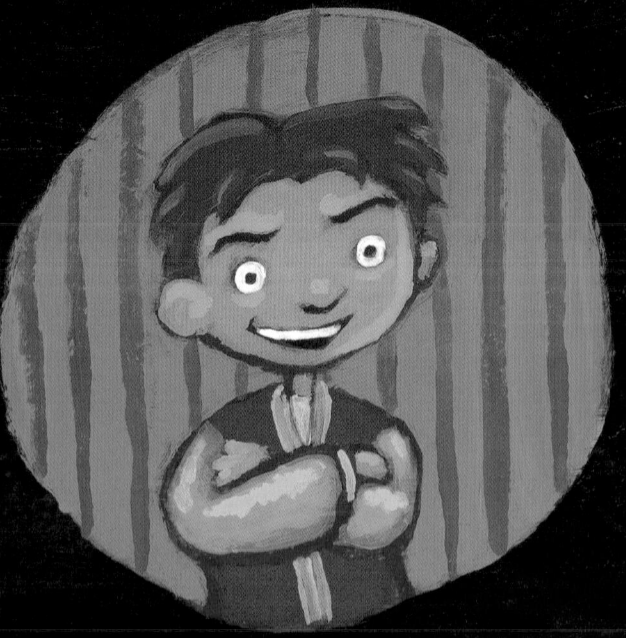

Annie's friend James nodded.
"That place is haunted, all right,"
he said with a shudder.
Then he grinned. "I *dare* you to go!"

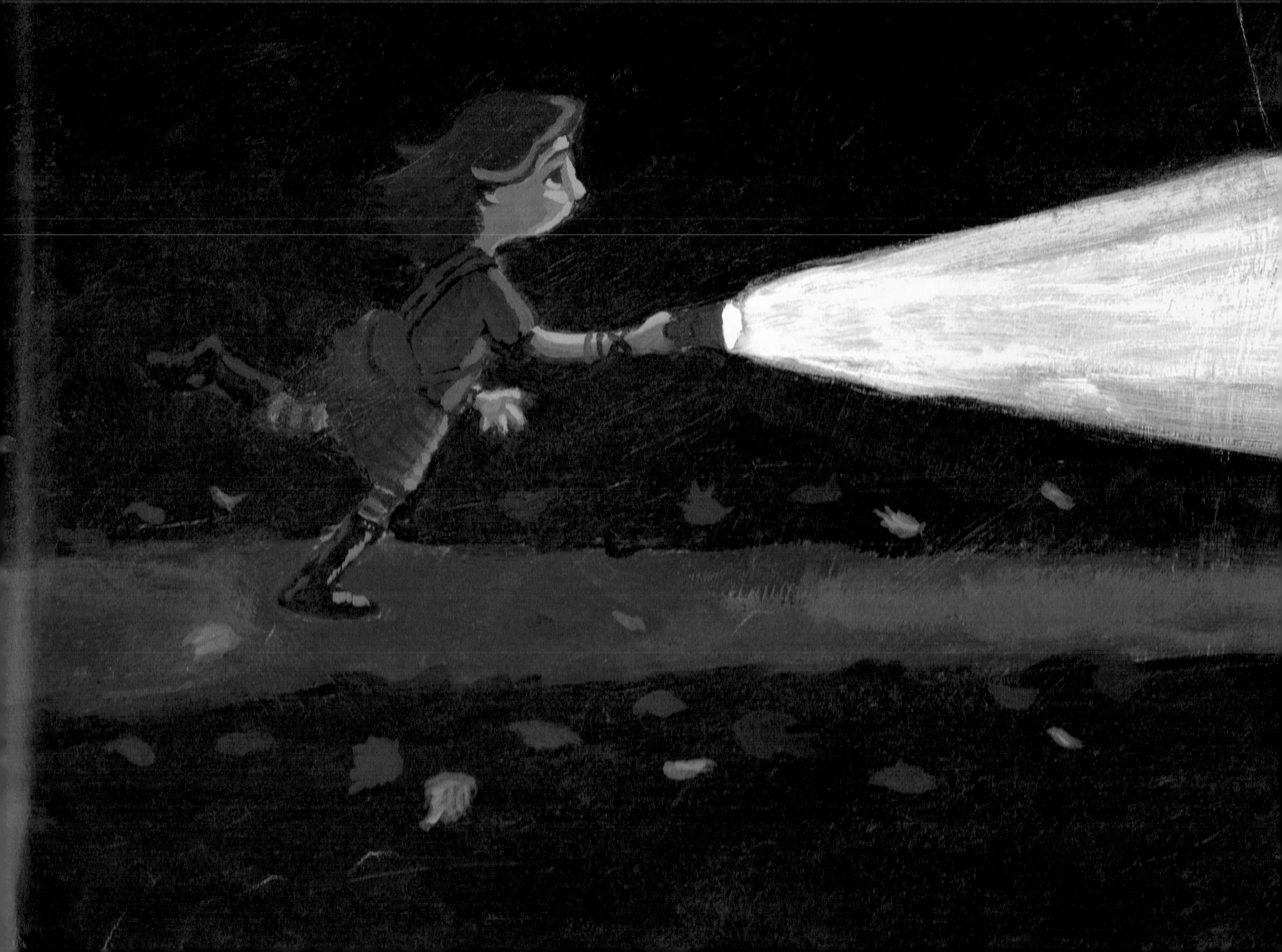

Annie was **warned . . .**

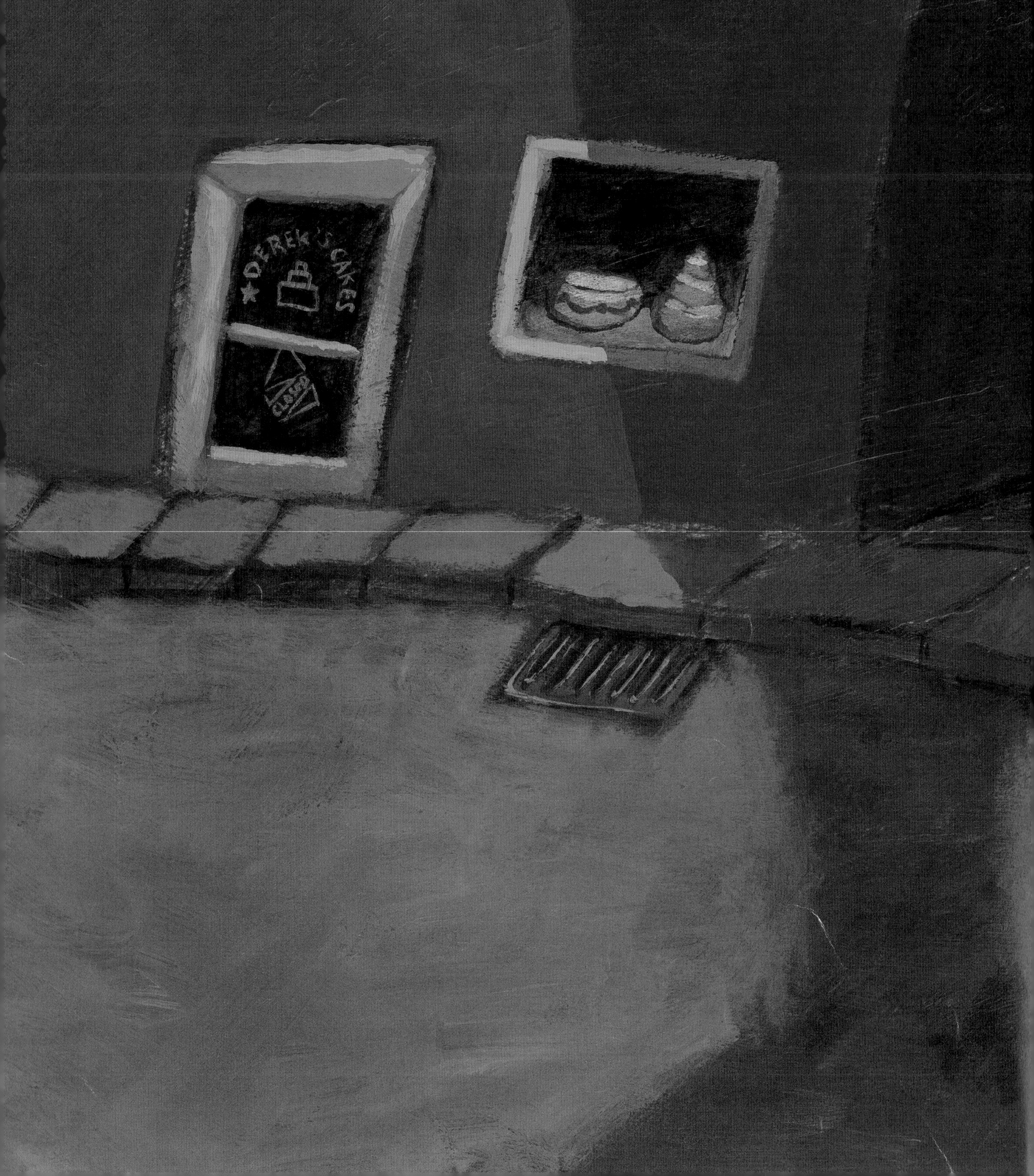
DEREK'S CAKES
CLOSED

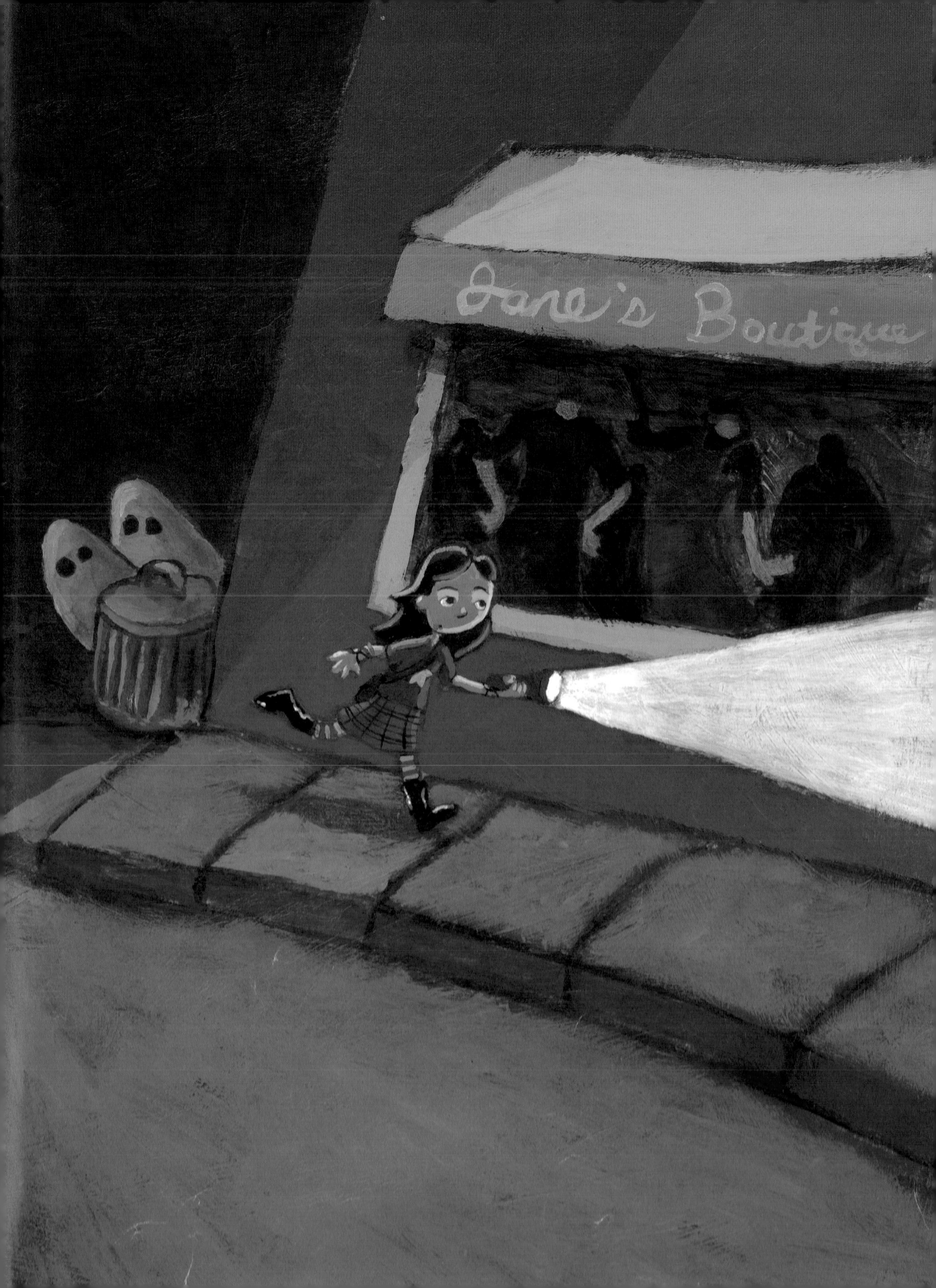
Jane's Boutique

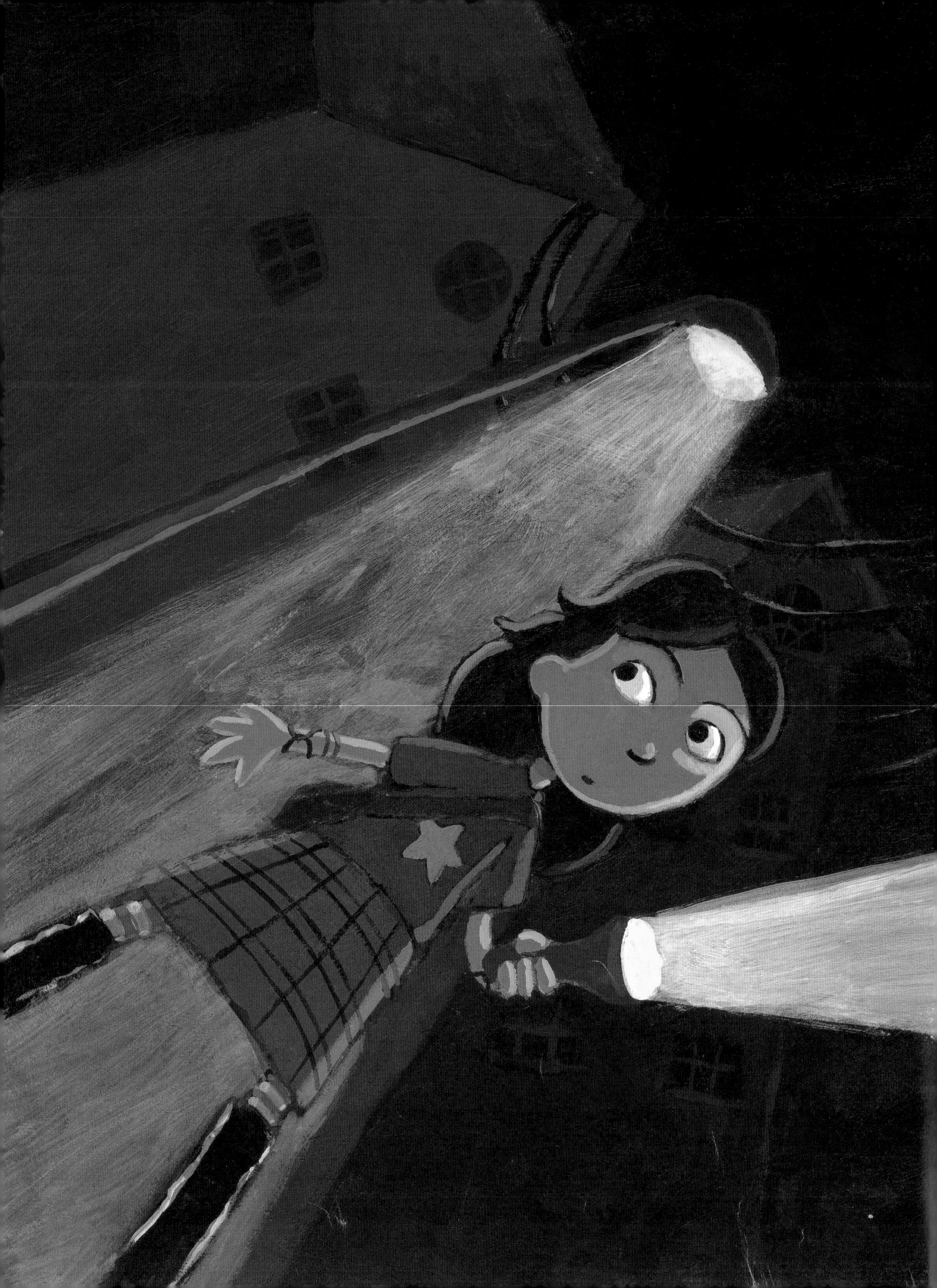

. . . but Annie wasn't **scared.**

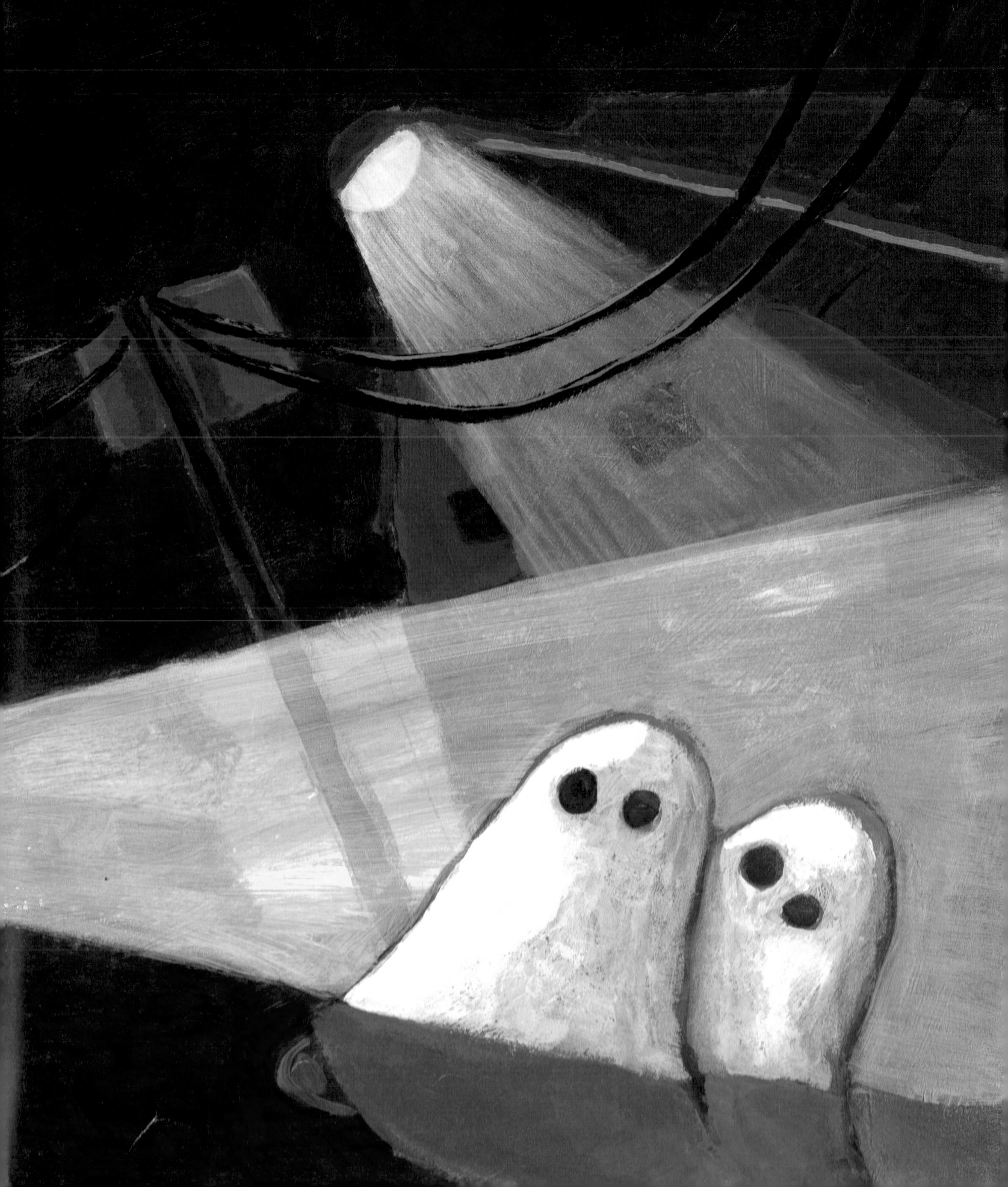

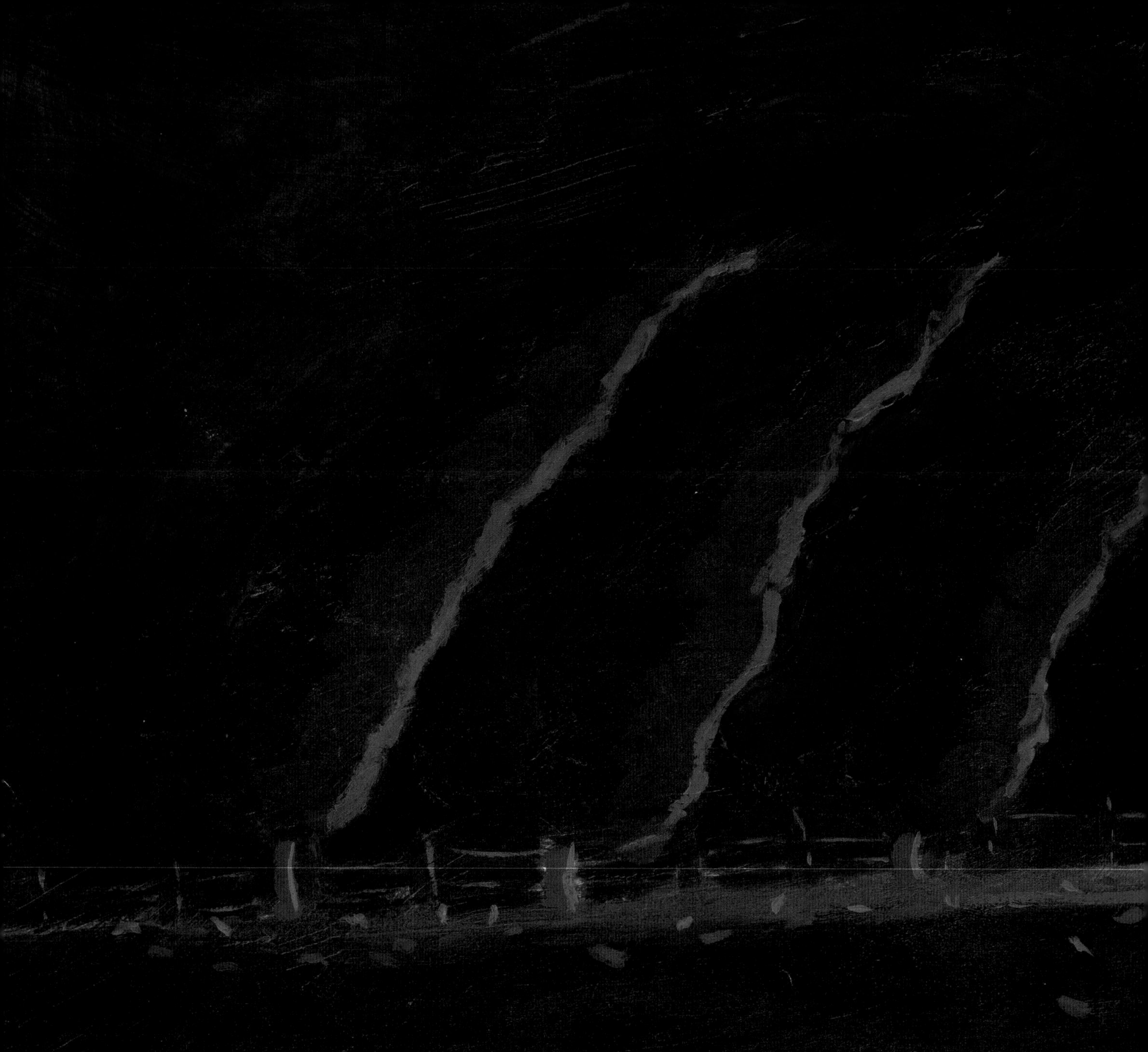

She stole down the quiet street.
The moon was shining. The wind was howling.
The tall trees swayed in the breeze.
But Annie wasn't afraid of anything!
After all, she was born on Halloween night.

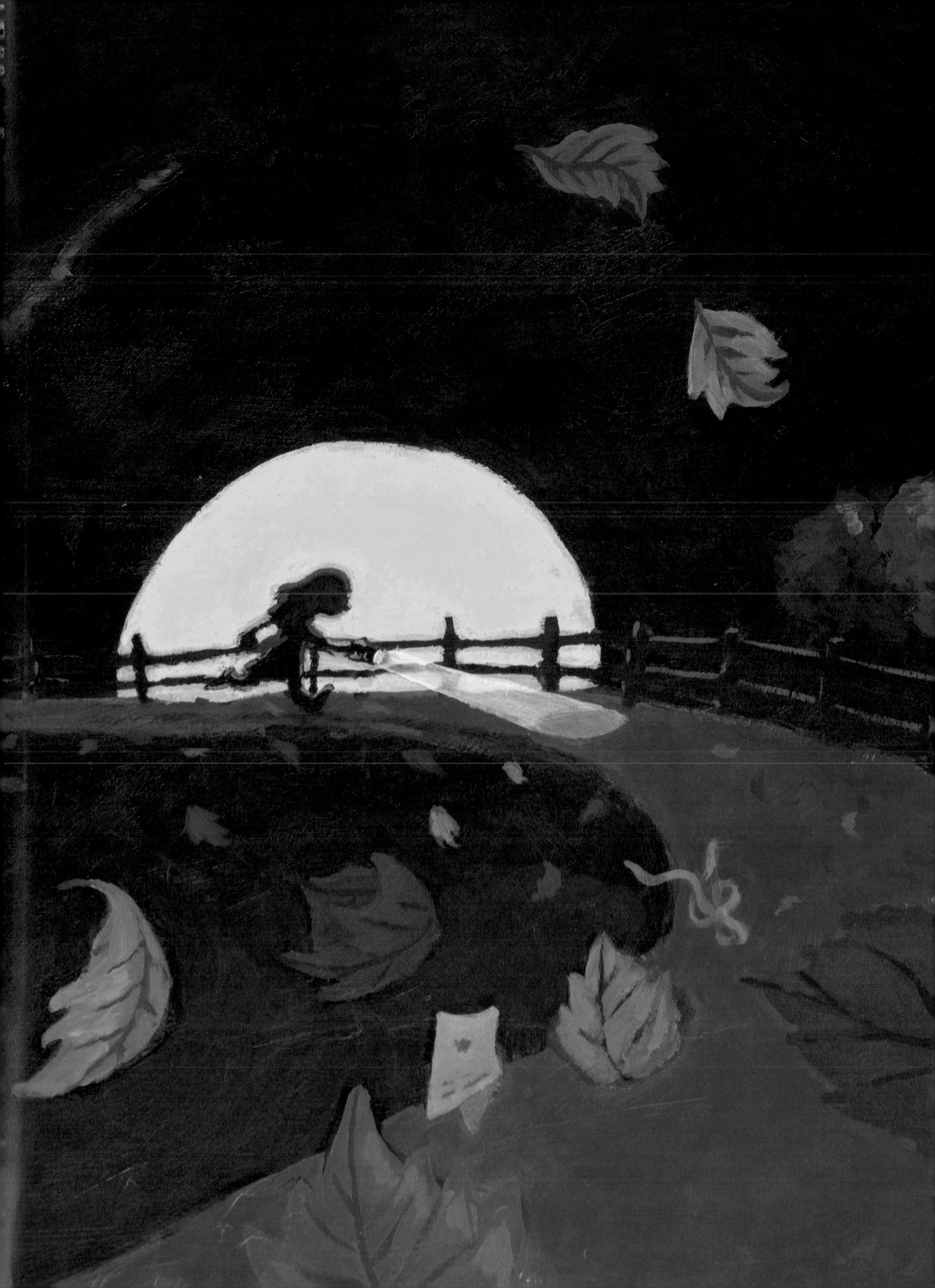

Out of the corner
of her eye, she saw
something black fly by!

Was it a bat?

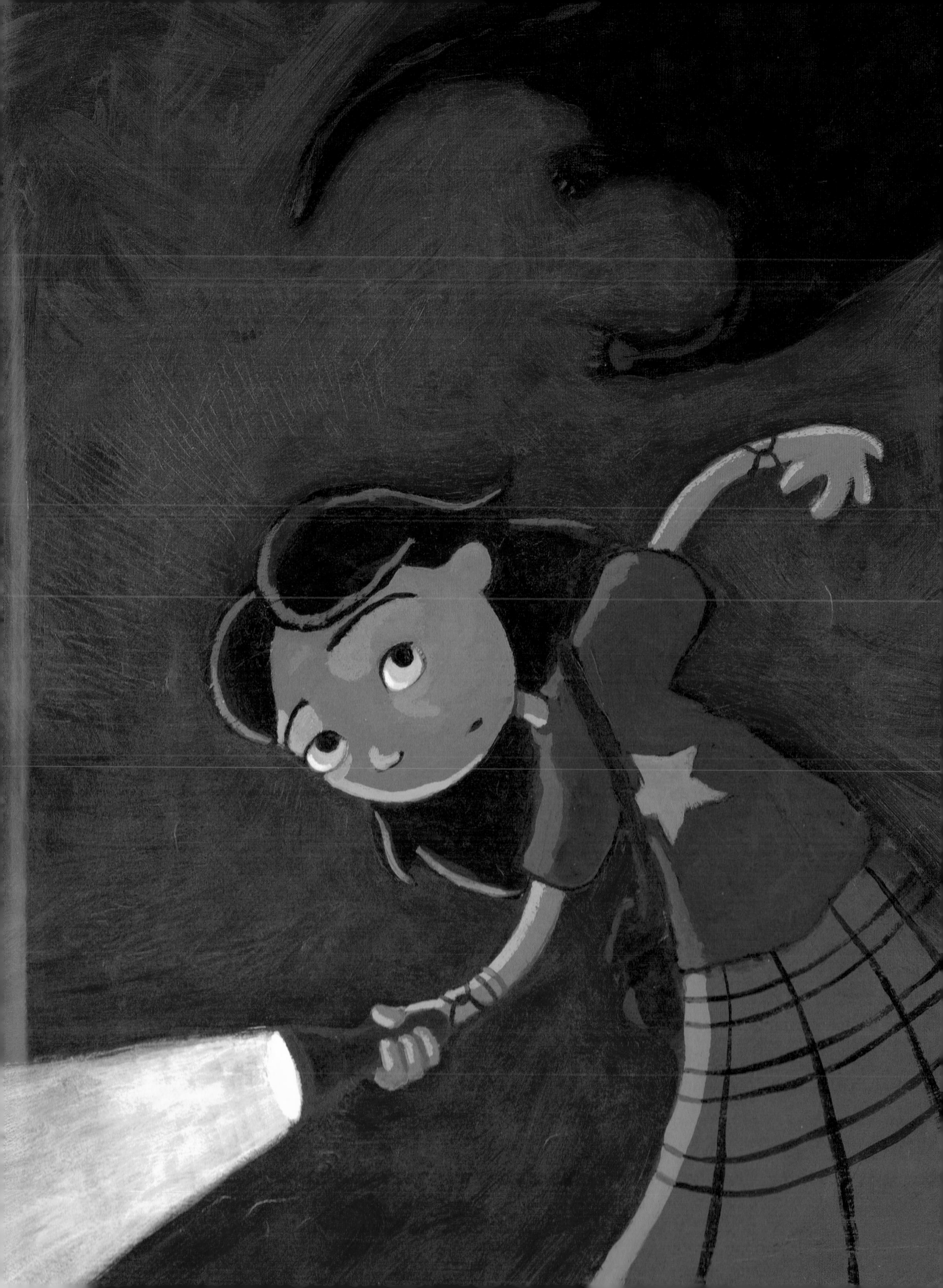

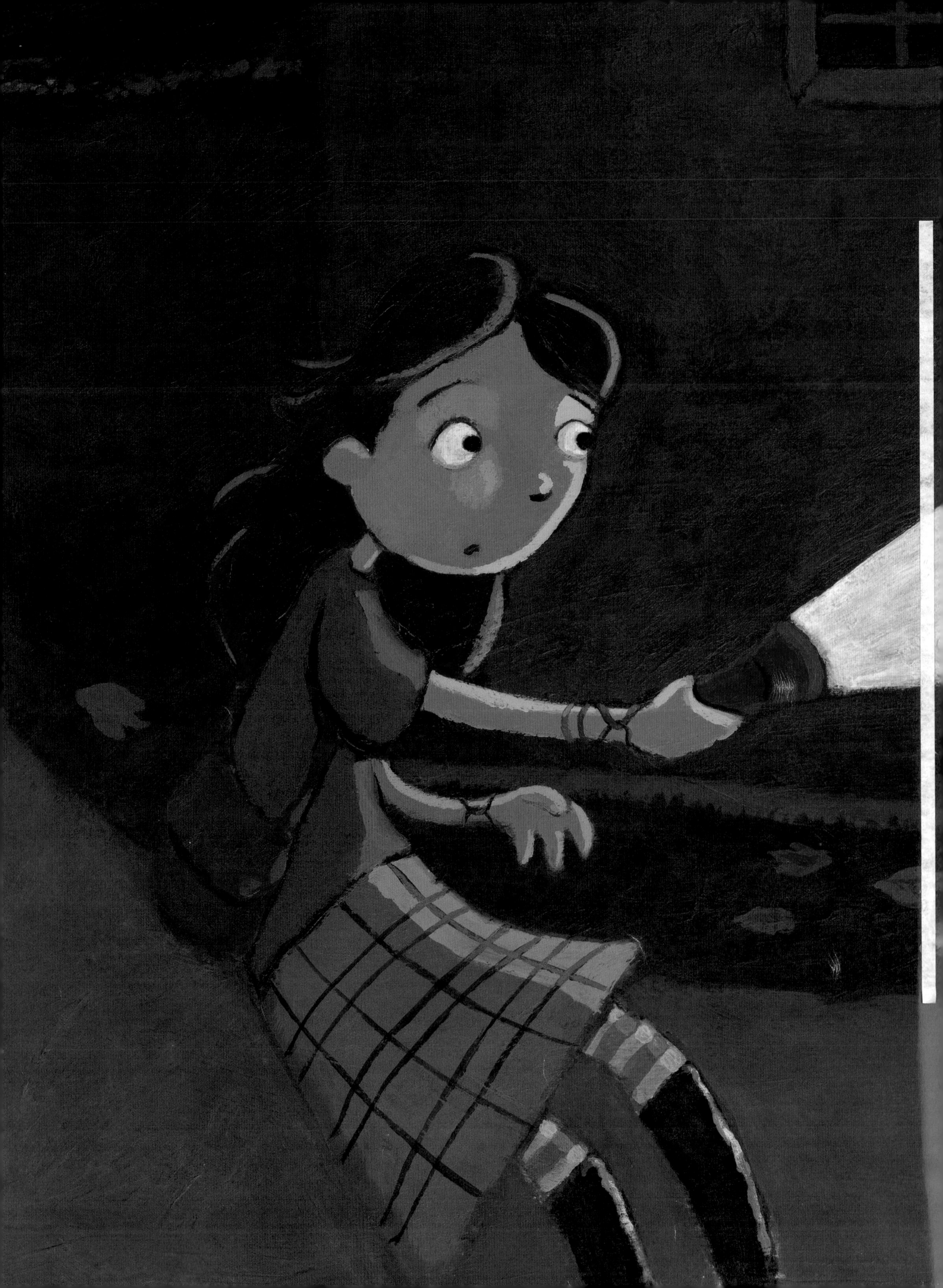

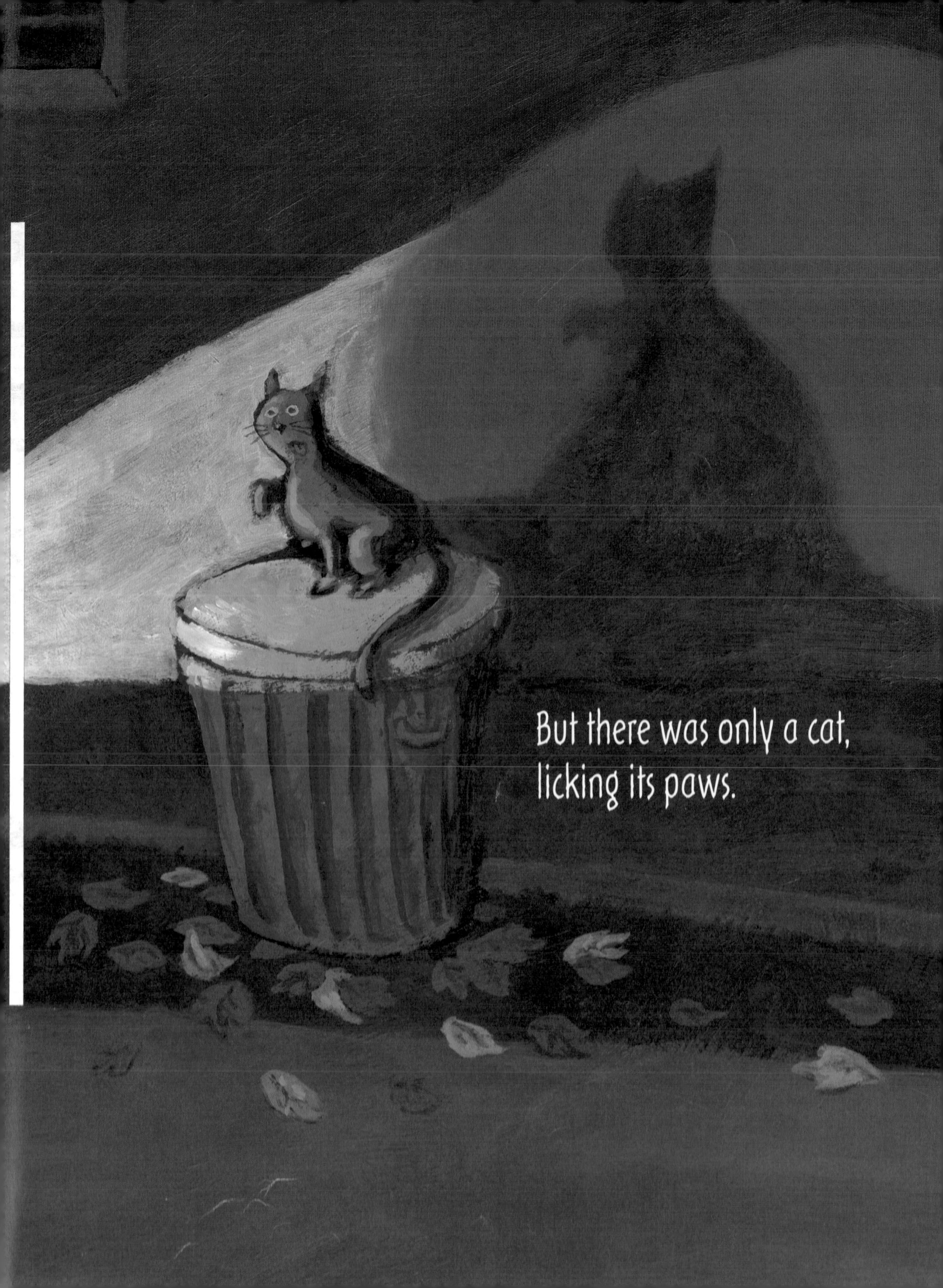

But there was only a cat,
licking its paws.

Annie turned the corner and crept across the churchyard.
Something tickled the back of her neck!

Was it a spider?

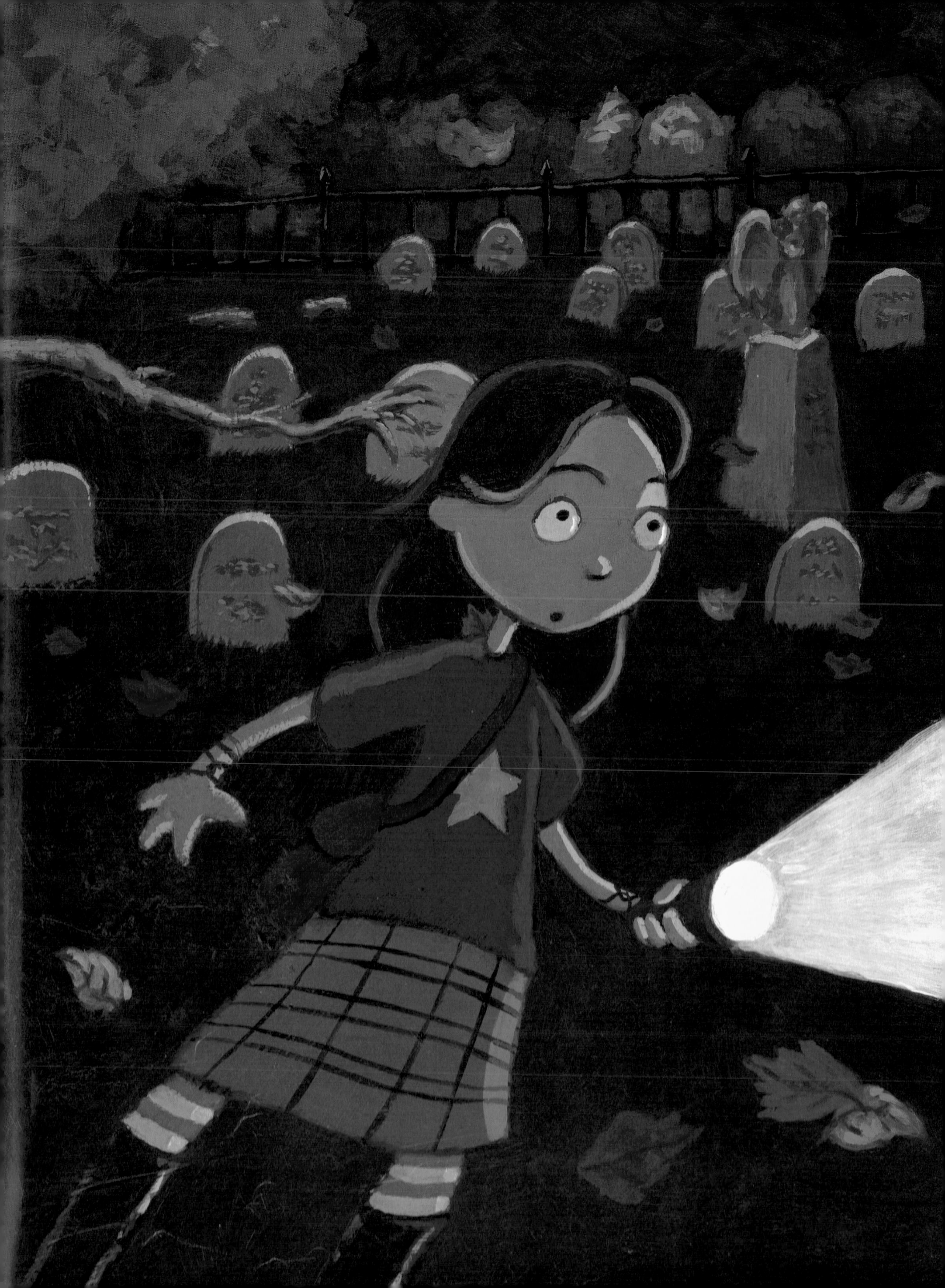

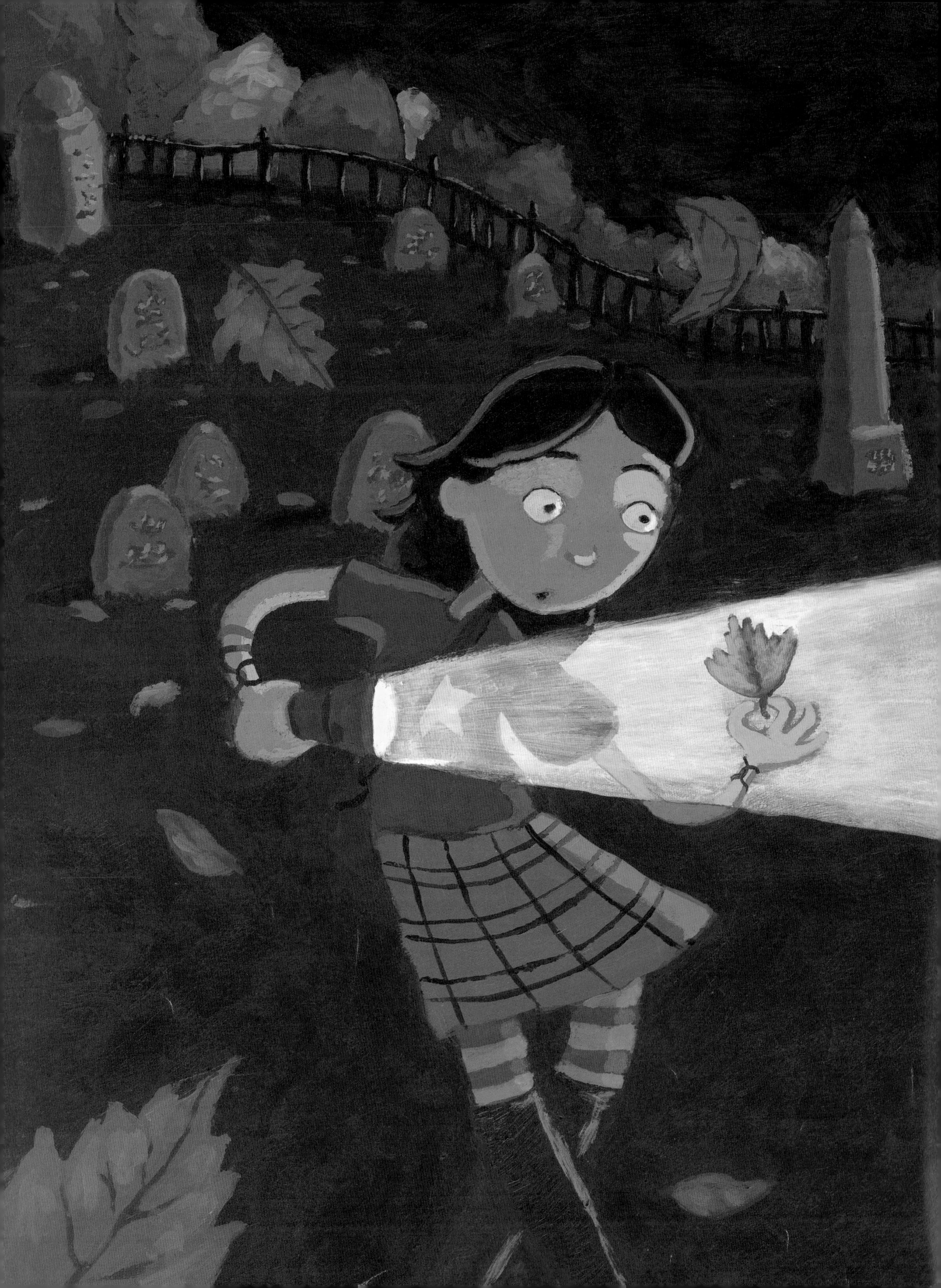

Annie spun around.
It was just the leaves falling from the trees.

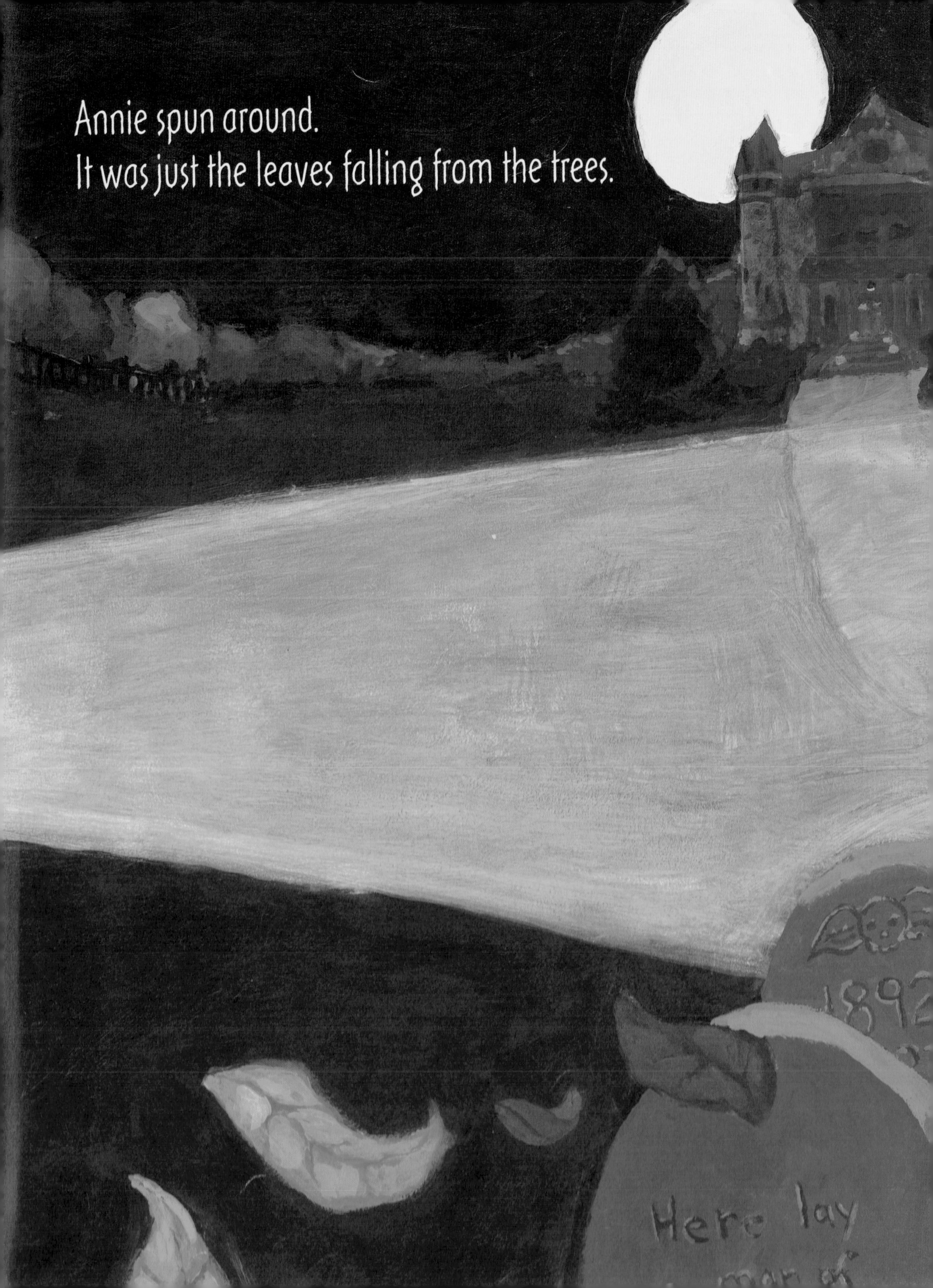
Here lay

The mansion loomed large in the night.
Annie thought she heard whispers.

Was it haunted?

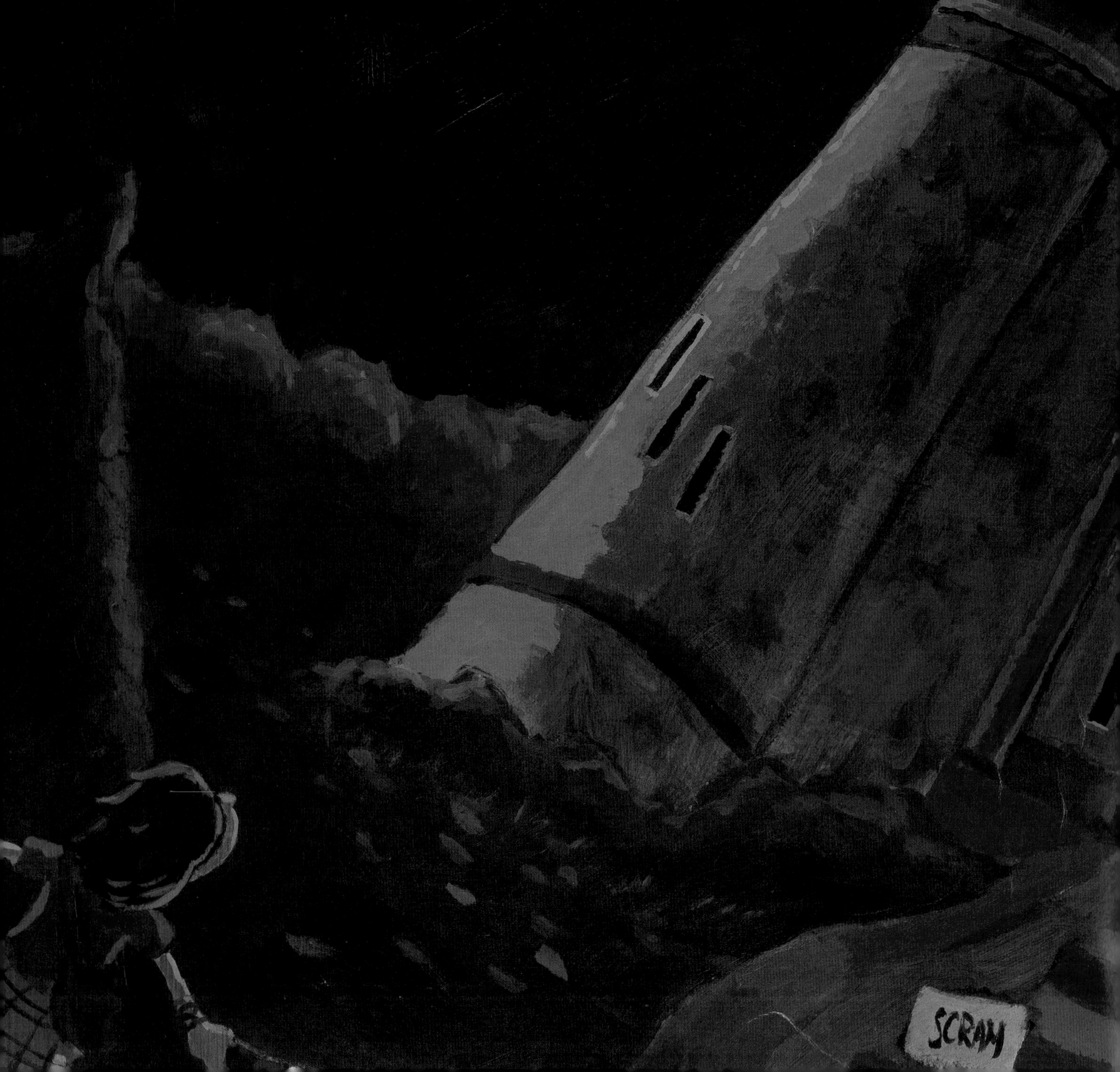
SCRAM

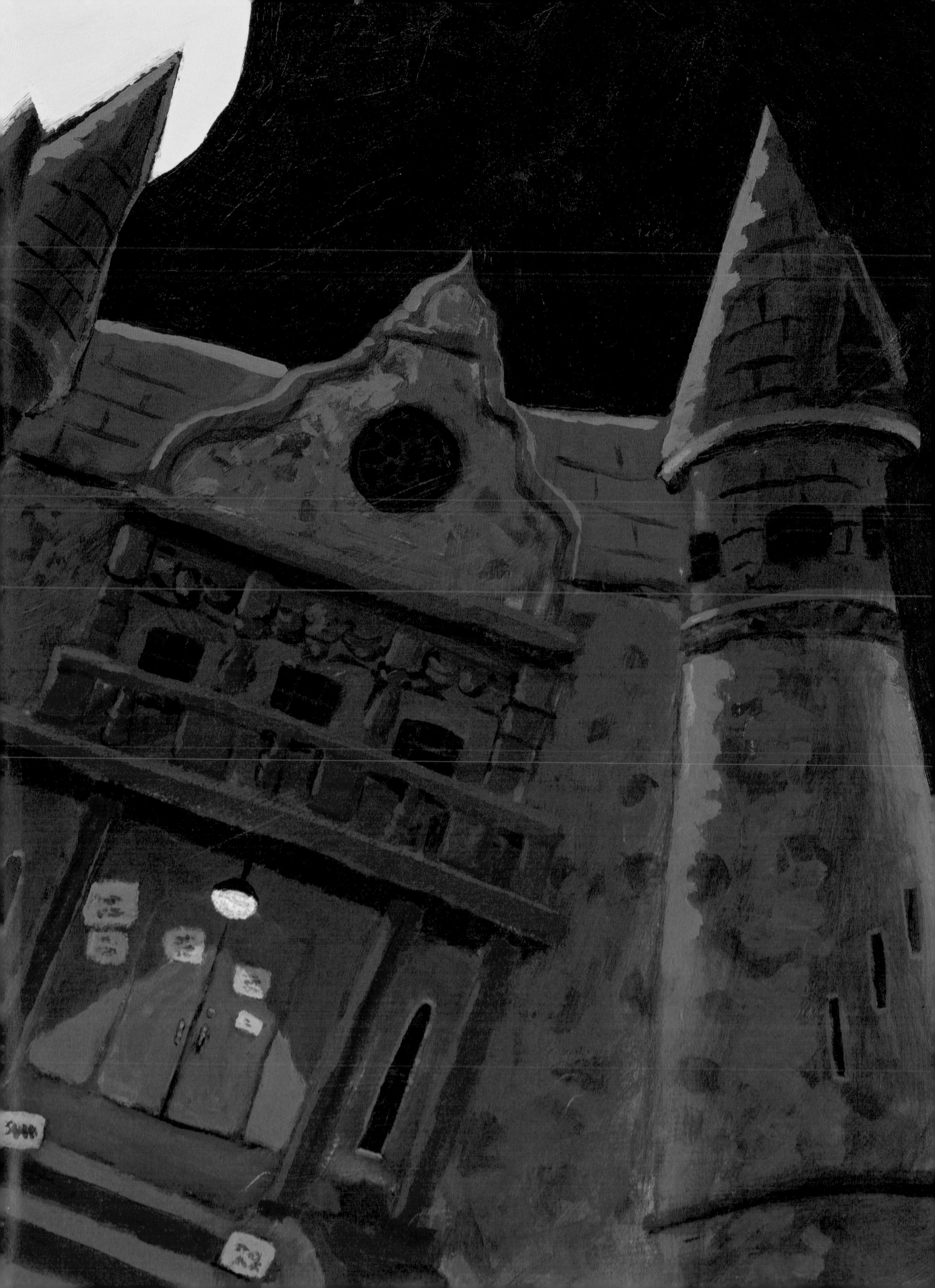

Annie took a deep breath
and began to climb the stairs.

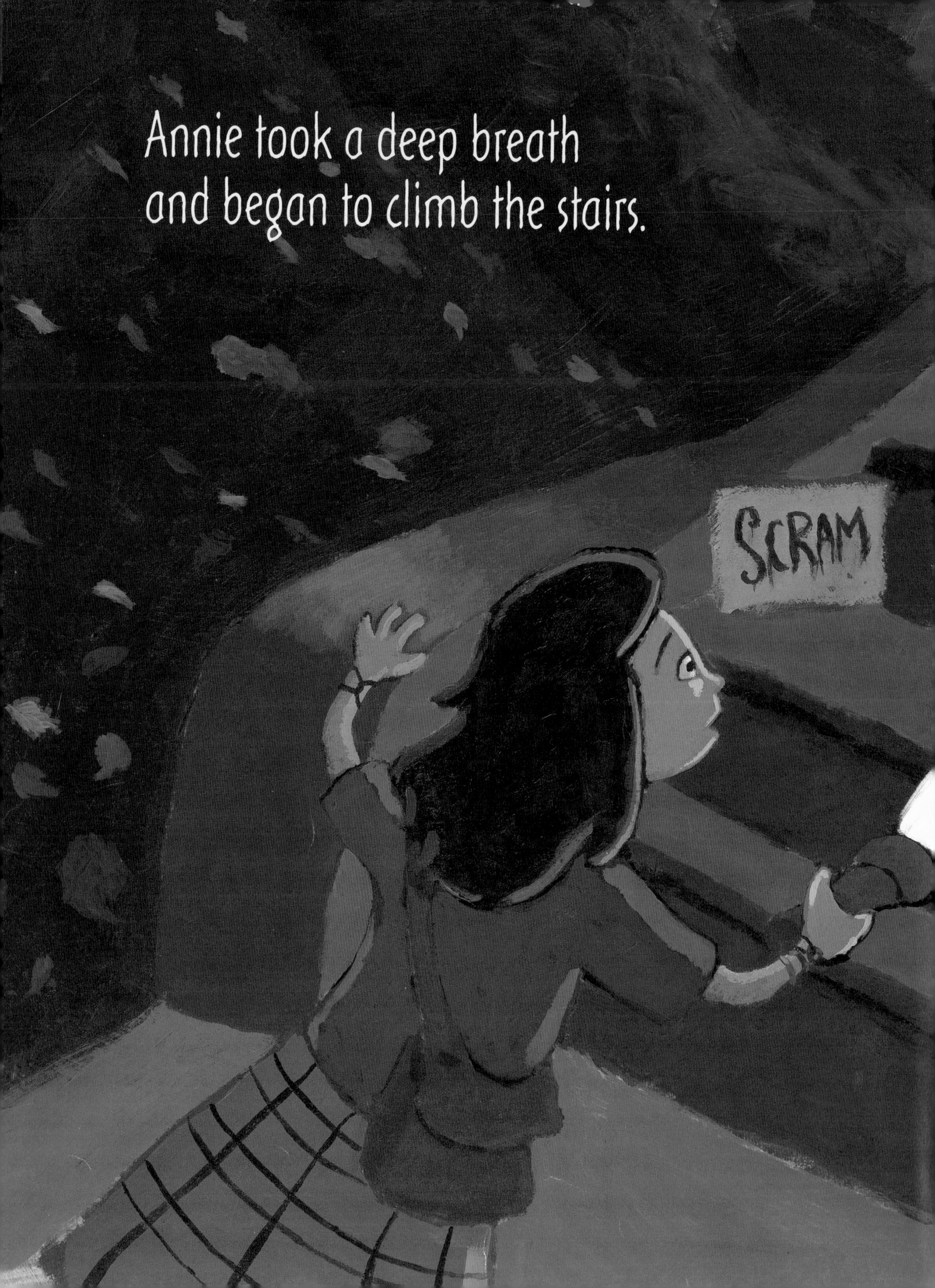
SCRAM

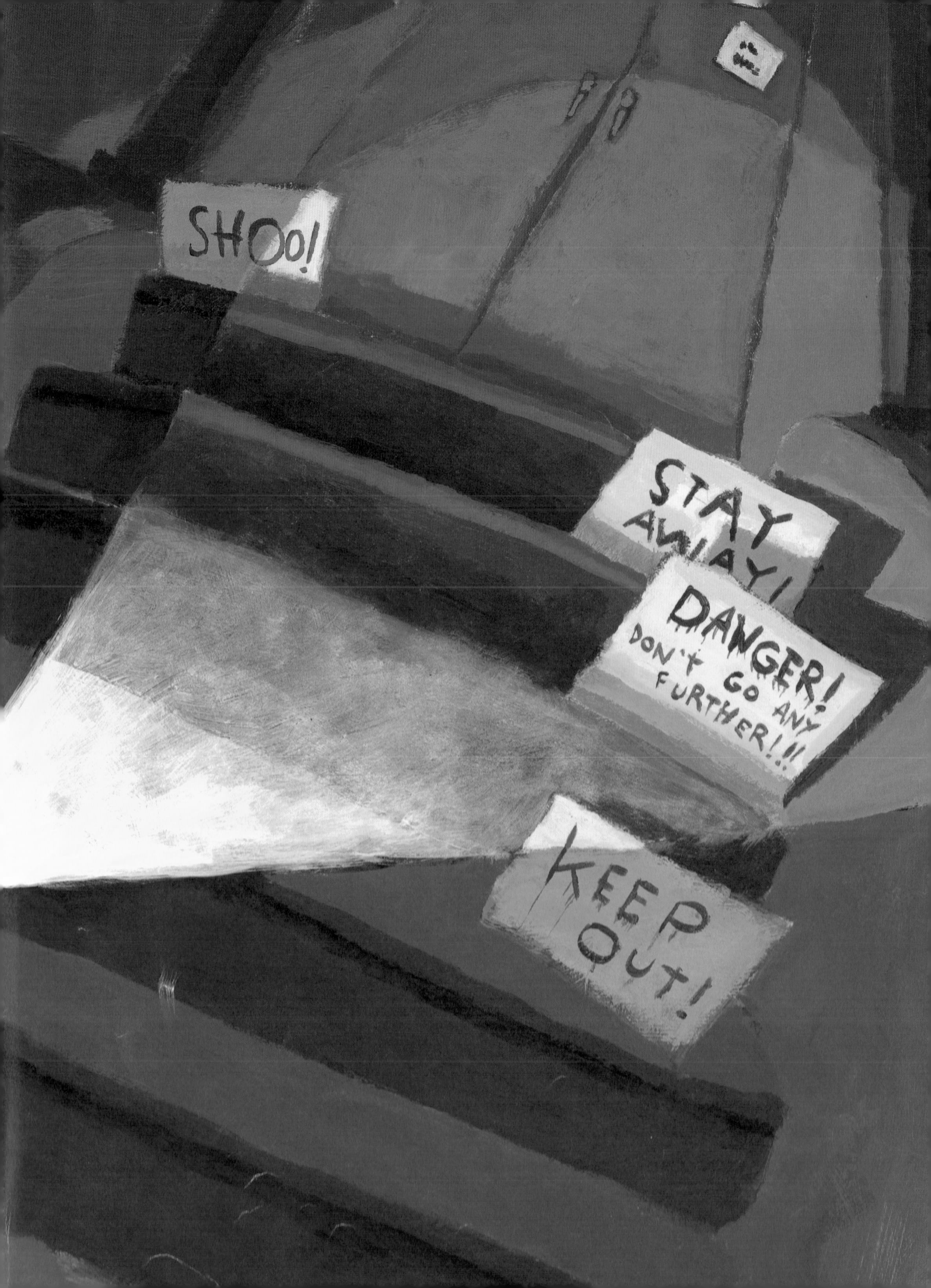
SHOO!
STAY AWAY!
DANGER! DON'T GO ANY FURTHER!!!
KEEP OUT!

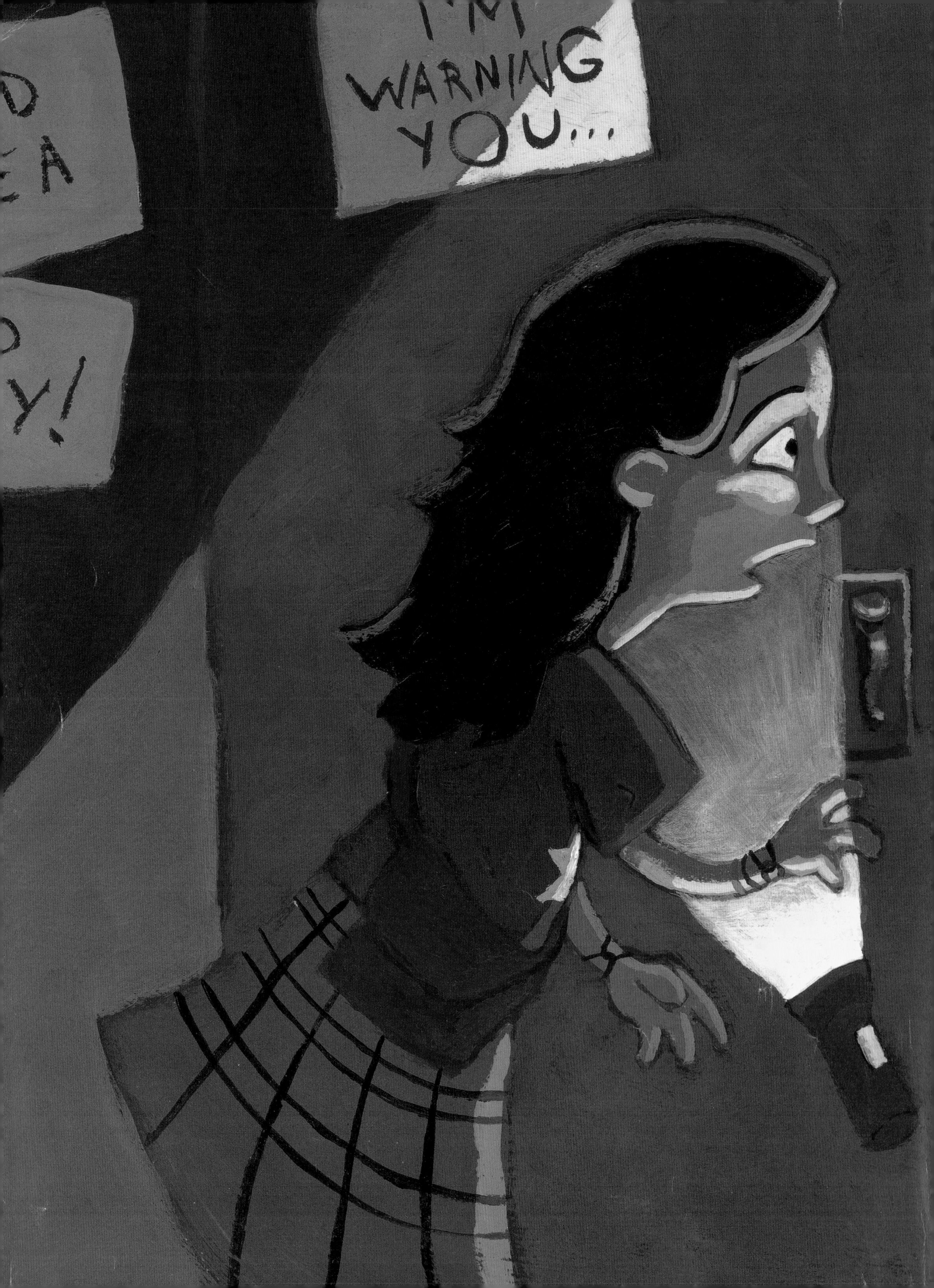
I'M
WARNING
YOU...

It was the best scare
she'd ever had.

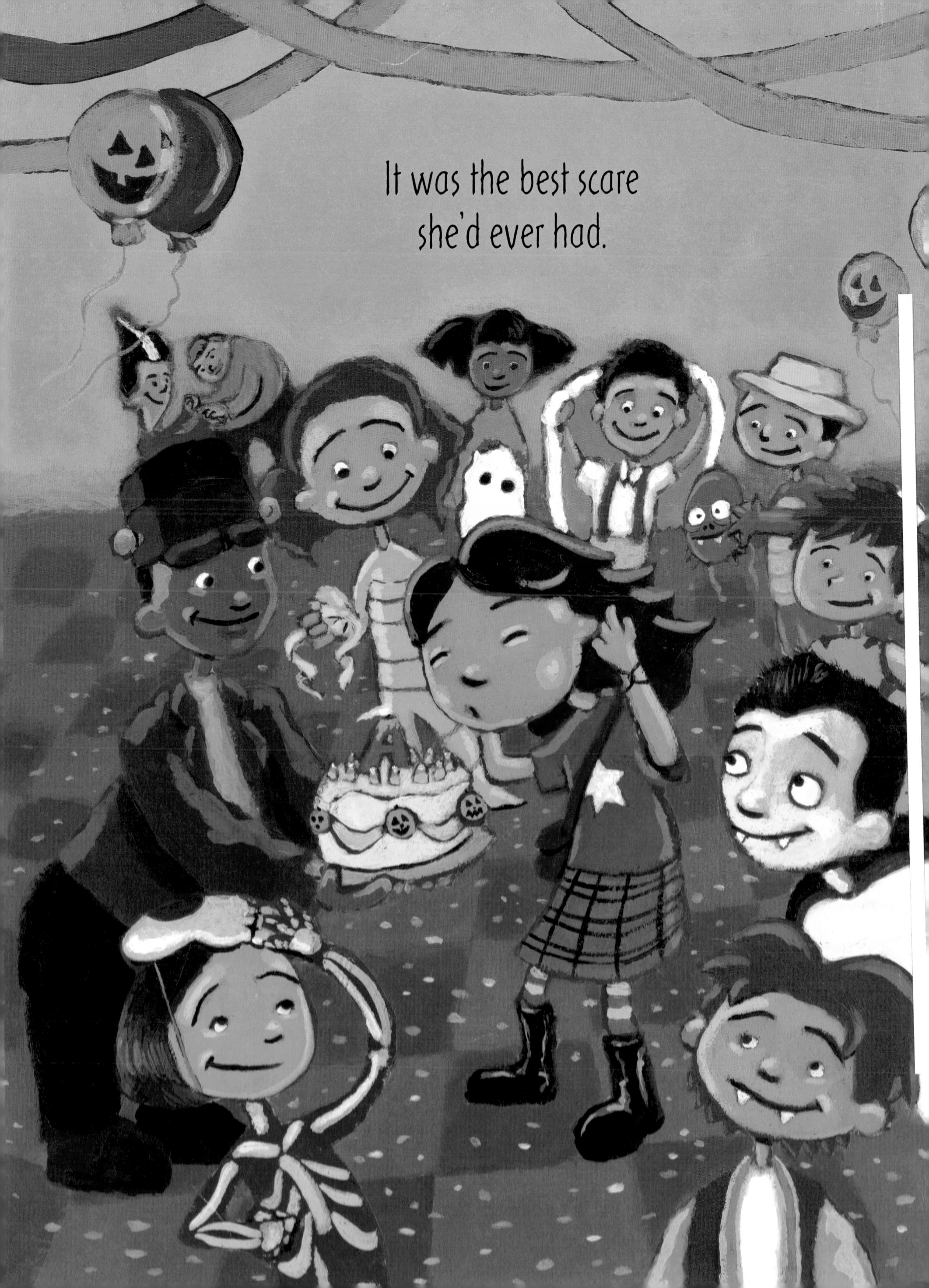

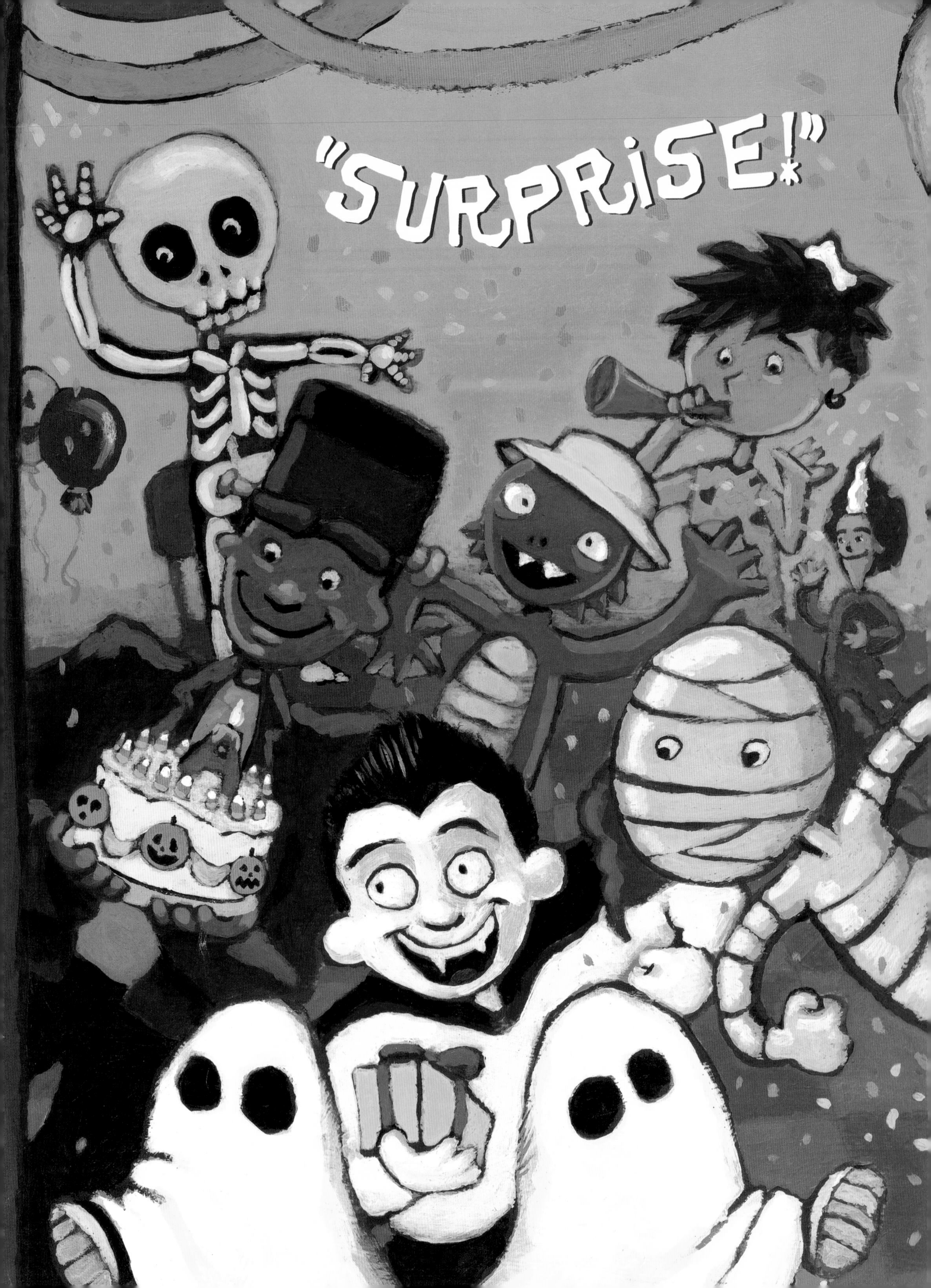
"SURPRISE!"

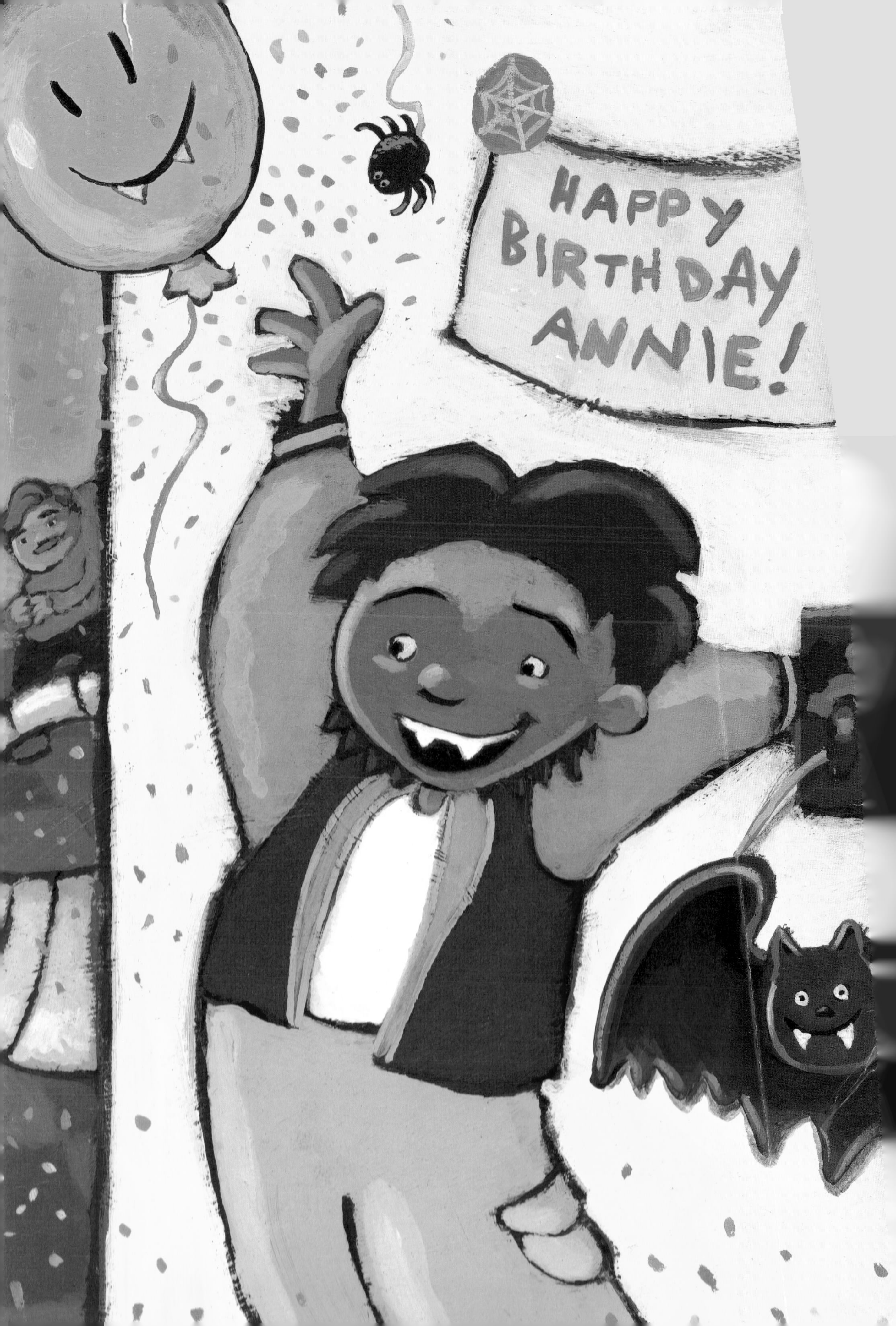
HAPPY BIRTHDAY ANNIE!

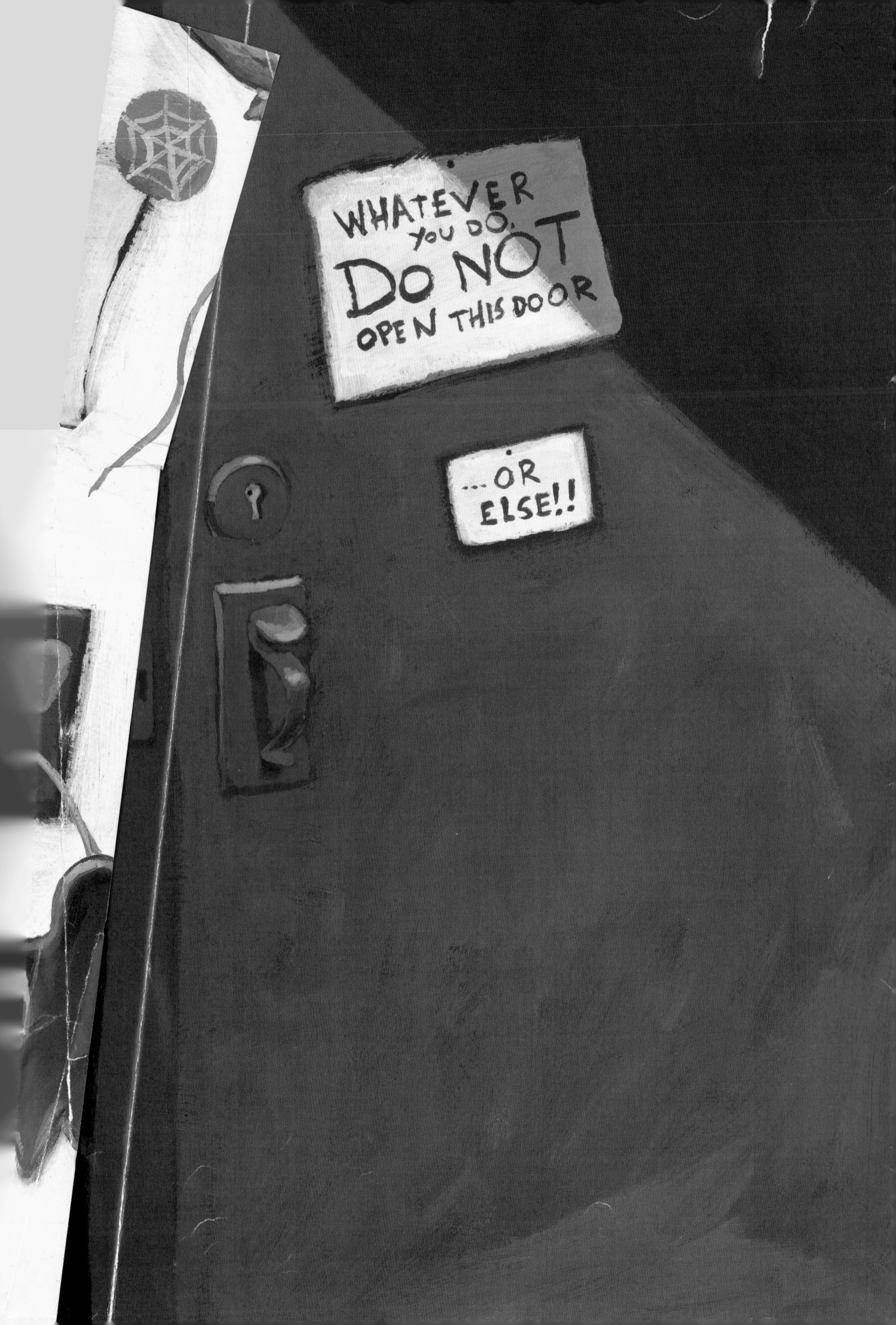
WHATEVER YOU DO, DO NOT OPEN THIS DOOR
...OR ELSE!!